© 2006 Disney Enterprises, Inc
Published by Hachette Partworks Ltd
ISBN: 978-1-906965-05-1
Date of Printing: November 2009
Printed in Singapore by Tien Wah Press
Based on the "Winnie the Pooh" works by
A.A. Milne and E.H. Shepard. All rights reserved.

Disney

Winnie the Pooh and the Honey Tree

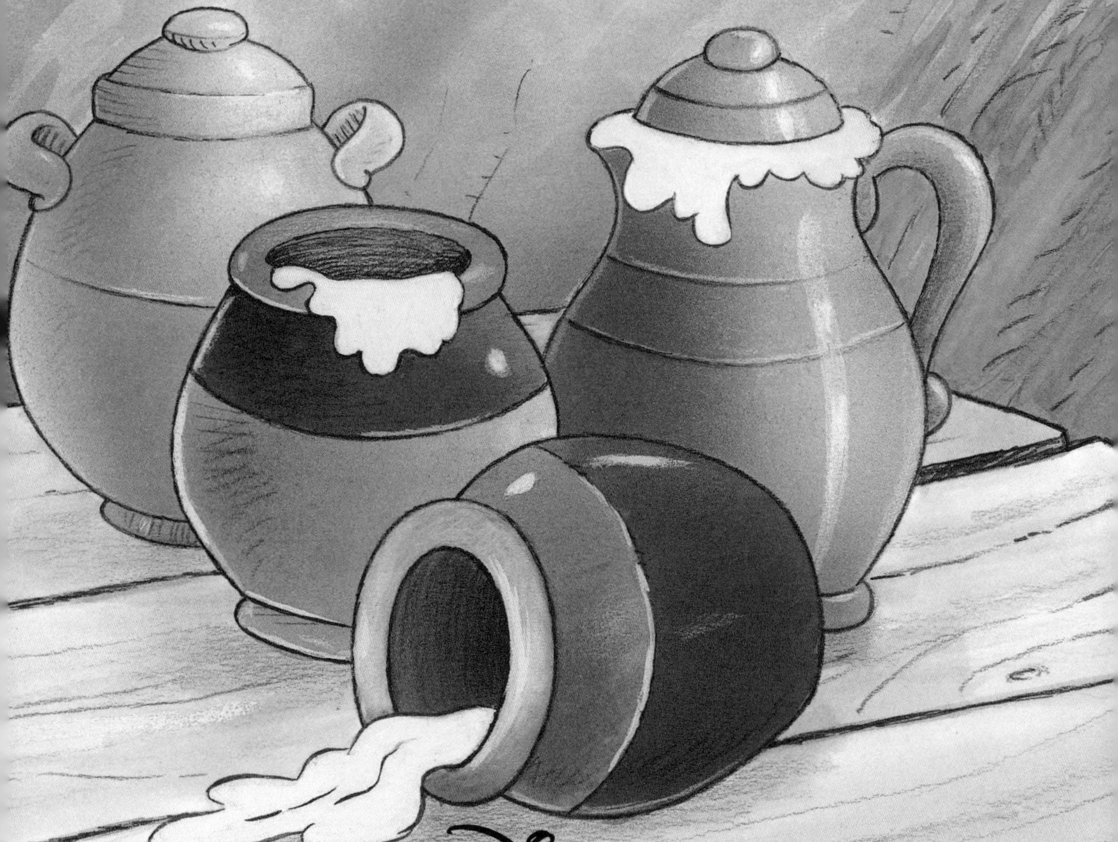

Disney

hachette

One morning, deep in the Hundred-Acre Wood, a little bear named Winnie the Pooh was doing his stoutness exercises.

"Up, down... up, down... up, down..."

Pooh felt a rumbly in his tumbly. Exercise always put him in the mood for food.

"Time for something sweet," Pooh happily declared.

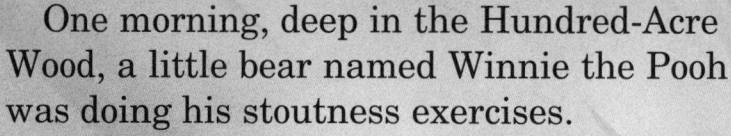

Pooh opened his cupboard for a pot of honey.

"Oh, bother!" Pooh cried. "Empty again. Only the sticky part's left."

Then Pooh heard a buzzing noise. Buzzing meant bees, and bees meant honey.

"And the only reason for making honey is so I can eat it!" Pooh decided.
Pooh followed the bee outside.

The bee flew high up into a tree, a tree filled with sweet, delicious honey.

With his tummy rumbling, Pooh eagerly climbed the honey tree. He climbed, and he climbed, and he climbed.

"Honey!" Pooh declared, reaching the top.
But the bees did not want to share with the bear.

They swarmed around Pooh until... *oh bother!* He fell! He fell – *oof!* – and fell – *umph!* – bouncing off tree limbs until...

...he landed – *whump* – right in the middle of a gorse bush!

"Oh bother!" Pooh cried. "I suppose it all comes from liking honey too much!"

Pooh was even hungrier than before. What was he to do?

"Think, think, think," Pooh thought.

Pooh was joined by Christopher Robin.

Pooh saw his friend's balloon and got an idea.
"May I borrow your balloon to get honey?"
Pooh asked.

"But you don't get honey with a balloon,"
Christopher Robin answered.

"I do," Pooh said, smiling.

Then Pooh rolled in a mud puddle....

… and took the balloon from Christopher Robin.

"I shall fly up into the honey-bee tree!" Pooh explained.

"But you're not a bee," said Christopher Robin.

"They'll think I'm a little black rain cloud," Pooh answered as he rose higher and higher.

"Silly old bear!" laughed Christopher Robin. "Good luck!"

"Hello bees!" Pooh said, reaching the top. He tried his best to look like a little black rain cloud, but the bees knew better. They angrily swarmed around him.

"Christopher Robin!" Pooh called down. "I think the bees suspect something!"

Then the balloon lost air.
It zoomed away and took
Pooh with it!

"Oh, my! Oh, help!" Pooh cried. "Christopher
Robin! I think I shall come down now,"
"Don't worry, Pooh! I'll catch you."

"*Oof!*"

Pooh landed right on top of Christopher Robin.

"I have come to a very important decision," said the bear of little brain. "I do not look like a little black rain cloud."

But Pooh did not give up. He set his mind
on honey. And honey rhymed with bunny,
and bunny meant Rabbit.

"Hello, Rabbit," Pooh said at his friend's
house. "It's lunchtime, you know."

"Oh, ah… hello, Pooh. So it is," Rabbit
stammered. "Ah, join me?"

"Oh, yes!" Pooh answered. "I'd love to!"

So Pooh joined Rabbit for lunch.
"Would you like milk or honey with your
bread?" Rabbit grumpily asked.
"Both", Pooh replied. "But
never mind the bread and
never mind the milk, please."

So Pooh ate, and he ate, and he ate, and he ate, and he ate, and he ate, and he ate, and he ate.

"Ah, would you like some more?" Rabbit asked, trying to sound polite.

"*Is* there any more?" Pooh asked in a sticky voice.

"No," Rabbit replied crankily. "There isn't."

"Then I must be going," Pooh said. "Goodbye Rabbit."

Pooh started out of the door. He tried wriggling forward. He couldn't. So he tried wriggling backward, but he couldn't do that either.

"Oh, help and bother!" Pooh declared. "I'm stuck!"

It was true. Pooh's tummy was too honey-full to fit!

"Oh, dear! Oh, my! Oh, gracious!" Rabbit cried.

"It all comes from liking honey too much," Pooh sighed.

"It all comes from *eating* honey too much," Rabbit scolded.

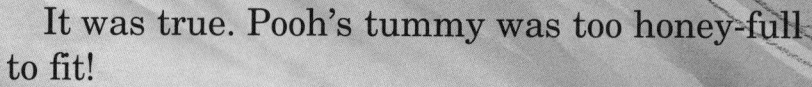

Rabbit pushed and pulled and shoved and tugged. But Pooh didn't budge.

"It's no use," Rabbit cried. "I'll go and get Christopher Robin."

Poor Pooh! He tried and tried to
squeeze through. He even tried to blow
out air like Christopher Robin's balloon.
But it didn't help. He was jammed tight.

"Well, if it isn't Pooh bear," said a familiar voice.
"Oh, hello, Owl," Pooh greeted his friend.
"You, sir, are a wedged bear in a great tightness," Owl said.

"Huh?" Pooh asked.
"You're stuck," Owl simply explained.

"This situation calls for an expert," Owl declared.
"Did someone call for an expert?" said a little
newcomer. "Gopher's my name. Digging's my game."
"It seems," Owl said, "the
entrance to Rabbit's
domicile is
impassable."
"Huh?" Gopher
asked.

"The bear's stuck," Owl explained. "What do you suggest?"

"Dynamite," Gopher replied.

"*Dynamite?!*" Pooh cried. "Oh, my!"

Just then Rabbit returned with Christopher Robin.

"Cheer up, Pooh," Christopher Robin said. "We'll get you out."

"Here, give me your arm,"
Christopher Robin said.
With Rabbit's help, Christopher Robin
grabbed and dragged and pressed and
pushed. But Pooh didn't move.

"There's only one thing we can do, Pooh," Christopher Robin declared. "We'll have to wait for you to get thin again."

"How long will that take?" Pooh asked.

"Who knows?" Owl answered.

    Rabbit did not want to look at Pooh's pudgy
posterior every day. But what could he do?
"If I have to face that thing," Rabbit declared,
"I might as well make the best of it."
    So Rabbit decided to decorate it. First he
added a frame.

"Very nice," Rabbit said. "Now for a splash of colour."
Then he placed some antler-looking sticks on it and drew a moose face.

"Not bad," Rabbit said, admiring his work. "It's rather good, I think."

"Oh, Rabbit," Pooh called from outside. I have a tickle in my nose. I think I'm going to... to... *ah-choo!*"

Pooh sneezed and messed up the moose!

"Why, oh why did I ever invite that bear to lunch?" moaned Rabbit.

Day after day and night after night, everybody waited for Pooh to get thin. The friends tried to cheer him up. Christopher Robin read stories to Pooh. Owl taught him long words.

Kanga and Roo brought Pooh a bright blue scarf to keep him warm.

Even gloomy Eeyore tried to make Pooh feel better.

"Well, it's better than dynamite," Eeyore droned.

One night, Gopher joined Pooh for a midnight snack.

"Ah, what sort of lunch is in that lunch box?" asked the very hungry bear.

"Oh, a pear, a squash and some honey," Gopher answered.

"*Honey?!*" Pooh hungrily asked. "Could you spare a small smackerel?"

"No, no, no, no!" Rabbit cried, running out of his house. "Not one drop!"

If Pooh didn't get smaller, he would never get out. So Rabbit put up a sign that read, "DO NOT FEED THE BEAR."

Then one day, just when Rabbit thought he'd never use his door again, it happened.

"He budged!" Rabbit said, pushing up against Pooh. "Hooray! Today is the day!"

Rabbit ran off to get Christopher Robin and the others.

"Everybody pull!" Christopher Robin yelled.
"Heave... ho! Heave... ho! Heave... ho!"
    Slowly, Pooh started to move.
But it was too slow for Rabbit.

Rabbit stood way back from Pooh... built up
all his strength... then as fast as he could...
ran straight for the bear's backend!

Pop!
Pooh shot out of the hole!
Like a big bear-bird, Pooh soared
though the air and...

... whump!
Right into the Honey tree!
The bees were terrified and
flew away.

"Don't worry, Pooh," Christopher Robin called from the ground. "We'll get you out!"

"No hurry," Pooh replied as he grabbed heaping handfuls of heavenly honey.

"Take your time, take your time!"